Cowboy Up!

By
Larry Dane
Brimner

Illustrated by
Susan Miller

Children's Press®
A Division of Scholastic Inc.
New York Toronto London Auckland Sydney
Mexico City New Delhi Hong Kong
Danbury, Connecticut

For Jean Ferris
—L. D. B.

For my husband, Mark
—S. M.

Reading Consultant
Linda Cornwell
Learning Resource Consultant
Indiana Department of Education

Library of Congress Cataloging-in-Publication Data
Brimner, Larry Dane.
Cowboy up! / by Larry Dane Brimner; illustrated by Susan Miller.
p. cm. — (A Rookie reader)
Summary: Presents a rhyming look at a cowboy's day at the rodeo.
ISBN 0-516-21199-4 (lib.bdg.) 0-516-26475-3 (pbk.)
[1. Rodeos—Fiction. 2. Cowboys—Fiction. 3. Stories in rhyme.] I. Miller, Susan, ill. II. Title. III. Series.
PZ8.3.B77145Co 1999
[E]—dc21

98-22307
CIP
AC

Printed in China.
25 26 27 R 20 19 18 17 62

Grab your hat.
It's time to go.

You'll need some boots for the rodeo.

Tickets

Off the fence.

Into the saddle.

SEED CITY
COW TOWN
Boot Valley

Cowboy Up!

Everyone skedaddle.

BOUNCE!

BOUND!

SPRING
AROUND!

THROW!

THUMP!

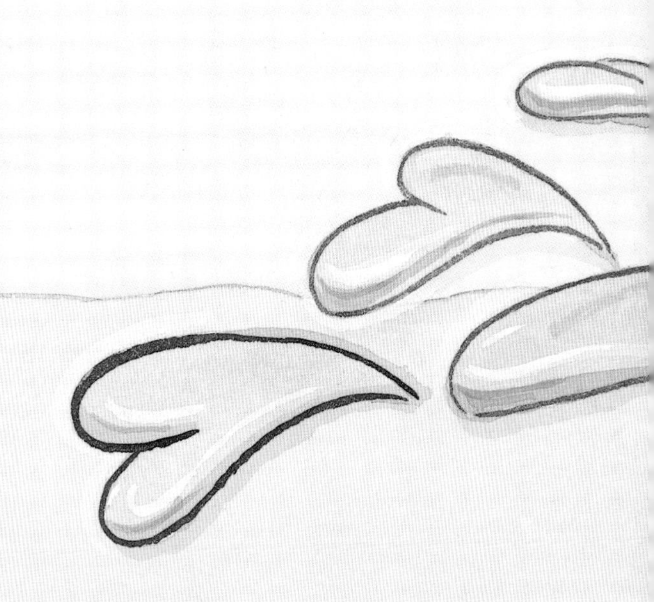

What a bump!

Rope a calf.

THE FARM
Fresh Goat Milk

Tie a goat.

WESTERN
WINNER

Rodeo's over.

Get your coat.

Word List (39 words)

a	fence	off	throw
around	for	over	thump
boots	get	rodeo	tie
bounce	go	rodeo's	time
bound	goat	rope	to
bump	grab	saddle	up
calf	hat	skedaddle	what
coat	into	some	you'll
cowboy	it's	spring	your
everyone	need	the	

About the Author

Larry Dane Brimner writes on a wide range of topics, from picture book and middle-grade fiction to young adult nonfiction. He has written many Rookie Readers, including *Lightning Liz*, *Dinosaurs Dance*, *Aggie and Will*, and *Nana's Hog*. Mr. Brimner is also the author of *E-mail* and *The World Wide Web* for Children's Press and the award-winning *Merry Christmas, Old Armadillo* (Boyds Mills Press). He lives in the southwest region of the United States.

About the Illustrator

Susan Miller has been a freelance children's illustrator for more than ten years and has illustrated numerous books and materials for children. She has illustrated *Nana's Hog* in the Rookie Reader series. Working in her home studio in the rural Litchfield Hills of Connecticut, she lives with her husband and two school-age children. They provide her endless opportunities for inspiration.